A GIFT OF READING
from
IMMANUEL CHURCH of SARATOGA

WWW.ILCSARATOGA.ORG   408-867-0822

This Book Belongs To:

_____

The Sleepy Little Star

written by **Kymberli W. Brady**
illustrated by Eddie Moreno

ISBN Number: 0-9711758-0-2

Summary:
A little star, like most children, doesn't want to go to bed,
and learns the importance of getting a good nights sleep.
For without it, he will surely lose his glow.

Printed in Korea.

get graphic publishing
a division of Kymzinn, Inc.

www.kymzinn.com

This is a very unique book in that it can be read two ways:

In its entirety, the story and dialogue between Sleepy and Papa Moon will be a magical journey into the life of this little star, and a joy to read to any child.

For a shorter, more poetic version, try reading only Papa Moon's quotes in blue.

To Cole,
My shining little star...
This book is my
gift of light to you.

Very early one morning in the village of Constellation, all the little stars were getting ready for bed. Sleepy, a stubborn little star, sat with his arms crossed tightly, not at all interested in his approaching bedtime. Determined as he was, Papa Moon could see the little star's glow beginning to fade, so he went over to him, scooped him gently into his lap, and said,

"Hey there sleepy little star, why are you still awake?
All stars must rest you know, for Heaven's precious sake."

"But Papa," Sleepy said, "I'm not at all tired. All the little boys and girls down below are just beginning their day. I want to stay up and watch them play."

Papa Moon realized that he needed to show this little star how important his sleep was, and how the children depended on him night after night to glow brightly. But his glow would surely fade away if he stayed awake. He took Sleepy down for a closer look at the town below and continued,

**"You need your strength
to shine so bright,
for you must light
the darkest night."**

"But I'm not tired," Sleepy replied, looking excitedly down at the town below. "Why can't I stay up Papa? Please show me more. P-l-e-a-s-e!"

Papa Moon smiled and nodded in approval. He told Sleepy to hang on tight, and away they went, into the night.

They arrived at their first stop where the brightest, most beautiful star Sleepy had ever seen was glowing so brightly she lit up the night sky.

Papa Moon explained further,

"God has given you a job to do, as He did the Christmas Star, who led the way for Kings in search of someone special from afar."

"Wow," Sleepy thought, his eyes fixed on the glorious light. "I wonder if I will ever grow up to shine so brightly and have such an important job."

Then, as quickly as they had arrived, they were on their way again.

They stopped over a lush, tree-covered area. Sleepy noticed another brightly lit star, shining down on some children hiking in the woods. "Wow those kids really need that star find their way home," he thought.

Papa Moon continued,

"And the great North Star, like a compass of gold, who leads the lost through dangers untold."

Sleepy was always too busy playing with the other stars to notice that boys and girls everywhere looked up to them. But why did he still have to go to sleep if he had a job to do?

Just then, Papa Moon whooshed him down to a beautiful park, where children were playing everywhere.

"While you sleep, the children will play, and fill their day with fun."

**"Then you'll awake,
your glow restored,
by the time their day
is done."**

Now Sleepy was beginning
to understand. If he got his
sleep, his glow would get
bright again. And if he didn't,
it would fade away.

Sleepy thought about it a
moment and yawned. He
thought he might be getting
just a little bit... sleepy.

Suddenly, he found himself looking in on some children as they were getting ready for their bedtime.

Papa Moon said,

"As mommy finds their favorite book, they'll settle in their beds."

"She'll read it as they follow along, then tuck them in and kiss their heads."

Sleepy knew how special mommies were, and he loved it when his mommy read him stories. But he still didn't understand what made *him* so special.

Hey, just what was his job anyway?

Papa Moon pulled Sleepy closer as if he had heard his very thoughts. Then, in the wink of an eye, they were outside the window of one little boy's room. There he sat in the dark, very much afraid.

Papa Moon explained to Sleepy,

"It is then that they will count on you to sparkle in the sky, and comfort them when they are scared of shadows passing by."

Sleepy never realized how important his job was before now. He was beginning to feel very special indeed,

...and sleepier too.

All of a sudden, he noticed lots of children looking up at him, with eyes all aglow and special thoughts in their heads.

"They will look at you and say as you twinkle in the night, I wish I may, I wish I might, have the wish I wish tonight."

"They wish their wishes upon *ME*?" Sleepy asked.

Papa Moon smiled and nodded at his little star, now beaming with pride.

Then he placed his finger over his lips, urging Sleepy to be extra quiet as they journeyed to their next stop.

...a best friend!

...a new scooter!

...Peace on Earth!

They found themselves back outside the little boy's room they had visited earlier. Only now, he was fast asleep.

Papa Moon leaned over and whispered to Sleepy,

"And when they close their eyes to sleep, they'll look for your soft glow. Then without another peep, off to Dreamland they will go."

Sleepy was now certain he had the most important job of all. He started to rub his eyelids, now heavy with the new responsibility he had discovered.

He yawned a very big yawn.

As he curled up on Papa Moon's lap, Sleepy noticed the sun beginning to peek over the horizon, filling the sky with the warm glow of a brand new day. Below, children were starting to stretch and stir from their sleep.

"So you see my cherished little star, all children count on you to guide them through their darkest hours, until their day dawns new."

Sleepy felt very special indeed, but was unable to keep his eyes open any longer. As he drifted off to Dreamland, he could hear Papa Moon whisper softly to him,

"But now it's time
to sleep and dream,
and rest your
fading light.
There's much to do
when you awake.

'Til then...
A kiss goodnight."

"The Sleepy Little Star"

Be sure to check out these other "Sleepy" items today!

Go to www.kymzinn.com

or call 888.806.STAR

for more information and ordering.

The Sleepy Little Star Book/Nightlight Gift Set

The Sleepy Little Star Nightlight (sold separately)

The Sleepy Little Star Nightshirt

and more!

Win $1,000.00!

In the first
"Sleepy & Me" Essay Contest

Theme:
"My Dream Adventure with Sleepy and Papa Moon"

CONTEST RULES:

Simply fill out this original form, and mail it with your essay of 600 words or less to the "Sleepy & Me" Essay Contest, P.O. Box 221164, Santa Clarita, CA 91322 1164. Entries must be the entrants own original creation and will be judged on the basis of originality, clarity of ideas, your child's involvement in the participation and interpretation as well as uniqueness of expression and relationship to the following theme: "My Dream Adventure with Sleepy and Papa Moon." Entries must be typed double-spaced or printed legibly and signed by the author. Entrants name, daytime telephone number and age must be printed on the back of entry. One winner will be selected from all entries received. Only one entry per household. By participating, each entrant accepts these rules and agrees to be bound by the decision of the judges, which is final. All entries will become the property of Kymzinn, Inc. and will not be returned. Contest sponsors are not responsible for lost, late or misdirected mail, or mutilated, illegible or incomplete entries. Winner will be required to sign and return an Affidavit of Eligibility and Release, within 10 days of notification, agreeing to: 1. The use of his or her name and/or likeness for any and all promotional or publicity purposes without further compensation, 2. Grant Kymzinn, Inc. and Get Graphic Publishing the exclusive and perpetual right to publish, edit and modify the entry for any and all future use without further notice or compensation to entrant, and agrees to sign all documents necessary to transfer copyright interest in the winning submission, and 3. Release Kymzinn, Inc., Get Graphic Publishing and its employees, affiliates and agents from any liability or damages resulting from entry in or winning this contest. Non-compliance within this time frame will result in the selection of an alternate prize winner. No substitution of prize will be permitted. All federal, state and local taxes applicable to the prize are the sole responsibility of the winner. This contest is open to legal residents of the 50 United States who are parents of children age 11 and under. Employees of Kymzinn, Inc., Get Graphic Publishing, it s affiliates, subsidiaries, advertising and promotional agencies, and household members of such employees are not eligible. All Federal, state and local laws and regulations apply. Void where prohibited. Entries must be received by December 31, 2003. One $1,000.00 prize will be awarded to the winning entry. Winner will be selected by March 31, 2004 and will be notified by mail.

For updates on the winning selection, publicity appearances, merchandise and other promotions, log on to:

www.kymzinn.com

Official Entry Form

My Dream Adventure with Sleepy and Papa Moon!

Parent or Guardian's Name _____

Parent's Signature _____

Child's Name _____

Child's age _____

Address _____

City/State/Zip _____

Daytime Phone _____

email _____

Sending in this original form constitutes your agreement to the terms stipulated in the contest rules. One winner will be selected from the entries received. Winning entry will be selected based on originality and relationship to the following theme: "My Dream Adventure with Sleepy and Papa Moon." No substitution of prize permitted. All federal, state and local taxes applicable to the prize are the sole responsibility of the winner. All Federal, state and local laws and regulations apply. Void where prohibited.

Mail to: The "Sleepy and Me" Essay Contest
P.O. Box 221164
Santa Clarita, CA 91322-1164

Sweet Dreams!